My Grandma Could do ANYTHING in the ADIRONDACKS

W9-BBU-330

by Ric Dilz

To all the Grandmas who love their Grandchild
to the mountain top and back!

RICDesign LLC
Boulder, Colorado

Illustration & Design by Nancy Maysmith, Helen H. Harrison & Ric Dilz

My Grandma could do ANYTHING...

Hi, I'm Cubby!

Can you find me in all the pictures?

My Grandma
doesn't
rock climb...

But she could!

My Grandma
doesn't
fly a rescue helicopter
in a gorge...

But she could!

My Grandma
doesn't do
a polar plunge...

But she could!

My Grandma
doesn't zipline over
a moose...

But she could!

My Grandma
doesn't sing
around a campfire...

But she could!

My Grandma
doesn't bungee jump
from a bridge...

But she could!

My Grandma
doesn't do
jumps on waterskis...

But she could!

My Grandma
doesn't hang glide over
the Adirondacks...

But she could!

My Grandma
doesn't ride
the rapids...

But she could!

My Grandma
doesn't do tricks on
a ski mountain...

But she could!

My Grandma
doesn't engineer a
scenic railroad...

But she could!

My Grandma
doesn't work as
a park ranger...

But she could!

My Grandma
could do lots of things,
but I'm so happy with
the one thing she does
the best...

White Tailed Deer

Can you find these animals in the book?

Bald Eagle

Wild Turkey

Owl

Eaglets

Woodchuck

Black Bear

Horse

Eastern Bluebird

Moose

Loon

Beaver

Brook Trout

Hummingbird

Rabbit

Squirrel

Raccoon

Skunk

Can you make these Adirondack Sounds?

 Have some fun and keep repeating until you drive someone crazy!

A Jeep on a trail
Beep-beep-beep

A scenic railroad
Choo-choo-choo

A water ski boat
Rrrroar-rrrroar-rrrroar

A loon on the lake
Ooo-OOOO-oooo-ooo-OOO

A pig on a farm
Oink-oink-oink

A motorcycle in a gorge
Vroom-vroom-vroom

An owl
Whooo-whooo-whooo!

A baby on a tour bus
Waah-waah-waah

A duck in a pond
Quack-quack-quack

A wild turkey in the forest
Gobble-gobble-gobble

What do YOU think?
Shout it out!
That's a Fact Jack!
OR
No Way!

Moose love to play soccer.
 You moose be kidding!

A roasted marshmallow with chocolate between two graham crackers is called a s'more.
 Yum, yum and more yum!

A baby deer is called a fawn.
So cute like you!

Park rangers love to hike with their pet dinosaurs.
 That's silly-o-saurus

Bears ski in the woods.
That would be beary awesome to see!

Trout love to sing "Baby Beluga" at bedtime.
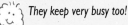 *A tuna fish could!*

Beavers have two sharp teeth in the front of their mouths and have flat tails.
They keep very busy too!

The Adirondack Park is the largest state park in the continental United States.
 That's more to love!

Share more laughs with these fun books!

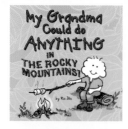

Available at
www.RicDilz.com

Published by RICDesign, LLC, Boulder, Colorado

ISBN: 978-0-9859684-5-8

Library of Congress Control Number: 2015916854

Printed in China